FRANKLIN WATTS
LONDON•SYDNEY

Chapter 1

Milly was a joker. She loved to play jokes on her family. One week, she decided to trick them every day.

On Monday, Dad was in the kitchen.

Milly was helping him to make pancakes.

"Oops!" Milly gasped as she dropped an egg.

"Oh, no!" cried Dad. He dived across the kitchen
to catch the egg. But he wasn't fast enough.
The egg hit the kitchen floor.

Boing!

The egg didn't break — it bounced!

5

Milly roared with laughter. "It's a joke!" she said.

"Isn't it funny?"

She picked up the egg and showed it to Dad.

"This egg's not real. It's made of rubber."

She bounced the egg on the floor to show him.

"Very good," Dad said, with a smile.

Chapter 2

On Tuesday, Milly scrunched up some newspaper

and pushed it into Grandad's slippers.

"My feet have grown!" cried Grandad

when he tried to put his slippers on.

Then he pulled newspaper out of one slipper.

"Milly," he said. "Did you do this?"

"Yes!" Milly laughed. "It was a joke!"

"Very funny," said Grandad, with a chuckle.

"Haven't you got homework to do?"

"No!" said Milly. She skipped away, laughing.

On Wednesday, Milly played another joke.

"What's wrong with the remote control?"

said Dad.

"I put sticky tape on it. That's why

it doesn't work!" Milly laughed.

"Hmm," said Dad, peeling off the tape.

"That's not very funny, Milly."

"I like playing jokes," said Milly.

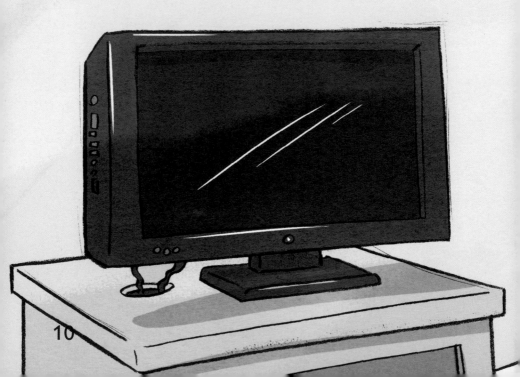

Chapter 3

At first, Milly's jokes had made her family laugh.
But by Friday, they were fed up of being tricked
all the time.

"Yuck," said Mum, pulling a face. "My coffee tastes awful. Someone has put salt in the sugar bowl."

Dad sighed. "We need to do something," he said.

"Let's play a joke on Milly," Grandad said.

He rubbed his chin for a moment. "In fact,

I think I might have the perfect plan."

Grandad told them his idea.

"Brilliant!" said Mum.

"Let's do it," said Dad.

Chapter 4

Milly's alarm clock sounded like a very angry bee.

She leaped out of bed to stop the noise.

She rubbed her eyes and stared at her clock.

"Is it Monday already?" she groaned.

"Wow. Saturday and Sunday went by so fast.

It feels as if we haven't had a weekend at all."

"Come on, Milly!" called Mum. "You'll be late for school."

"Hurry up!" shouted Grandad.

"I'll be waiting in the car!" yelled Dad.

"I'M COMING!" cried Milly.

19

She ran down the stairs.

But there was no one to be seen.

"Here I am!" she called.

The kitchen was empty.

Where was everyone?

"How odd," said Milly.

Then she heard a noise coming from

the living room. She pushed open the door.

Chapter 5

"SURPRISE!" cried Mum, Dad and Grandad.
Everyone was wearing pyjamas and
dressing gowns. They jumped up and down,
laughing at Milly.

"What are you doing?" asked Milly. "Why is
no one dressed? I'm going to be late for school!"

"No, you're not going to be late," said Dad,
shaking his head.

Mum sat down in an armchair and sipped a cup of coffee. "Mmm, that's nice," she said.

"Has anyone seen my newspaper?" asked Grandad.

"I said, I am going to be late!" said Milly,
pointing to the clock on the wall.

Dad beamed. "You're not going to be late,
because it's ..."

"SATURDAY!" they all cried.

Milly froze. She looked at the clock again.

She looked at her family. Everyone waited.

Then Milly began to smile. "You played a joke on me," she said. "And I fell for it!"

Milly laughed so hard that tears ran down her cheeks. Everyone else joined in.

"I've learned my lesson," Milly said,

when she had stopped laughing.

"There'll be no more jokes, ever."

Everyone looked at Milly in surprise.

"Really?" said Mum.

"I'm joking!" said Milly, with a wink.

"I might do one or two."

Things to think about

1. Why do Milly's family get fed up with her jokes?
2. Can you think which jokes are funny, and which might be annoying?
3. Why do you think Milly's family decided to play a joke on her?
4. Do you think Milly has learned a lesson?
5. Do you think Milly will play as many jokes on her family in the future?

Write it yourself

One of the themes of this story is being a good sport. Can you write a story with a similar theme?

Plan your story before you begin to write it.
Start off with a story map:

- a beginning to introduce the characters and where your story is set (the setting);
- a problem which the main characters will need to fix;
- an ending where the problems are resolved.

Get writing! Try to use interesting language, such as "alarm clock sounded like a very angry bee", to describe your story world and excite your reader.

Notes for parents and carers

Independent reading
This series is designed to provide an opportunity for your child to read independently, for pleasure and enjoyment. These notes are written for you to help your child make the most of this book.

About the book
Milly is a joker - she loves playing jokes on her family. But after a whole week of Milly tricking them, her family decide to play a joke of their own, and Milly learns a lesson!

Before reading
Ask your child why they have selected this book. Look at the title and blurb together. What do they think it will be about? Do they think they will like it?

During reading
Encourage your child to read independently. If they get stuck on a word, remind them that they can sound it out in syllable chunks. They can also read on in the sentence and think about what would make sense.

After reading
Support comprehension and help your child think about the messages in the book that go beyond the story, using the questions on the page opposite. Give your child a chance to respond to the story, asking:
*   Did you enjoy the story and why?
*   Who was your favourite character?
*   What was your favourite part?
*   What did you expect to happen at the end?

Franklin Watts
First published in Great Britain in 2020
by The Watts Publishing Group

Series Editors: Jackie Hamley and Melanie Palmer
Series Advisors: Dr Sue Bodman and Glen Franklin
Series Designers: Cathryn Gilbert and Peter Scoulding

A CIP catalogue record for this book is
available from the British Library.

ISBN 978 1 4451 6881 4 (hbk)
ISBN 978 1 4451 6883 8 (pbk)
ISBN 978 1 4451 6882 1 (library ebook)
ISBN 978 1 4451 7878 3 (ebook)

Printed in China

Franklin Watts
An imprint of
Hachette Children's Group
Part of The Watts Publishing Group
Carmelite House
50 Victoria Embankment
London EC4Y 0DZ

An Hachette UK Company
www.hachette.co.uk

www.reading-champion.co.uk